This edition published by Parragon Books Ltd in 2017

Parragon Books Ltd
Chartist House
15–17 Trim Street
Bath BA1 1HA, UK
www.parragon.com

T#554523

ISBN 978-1-4748-7814-2

Printed in China

My Book of
EVERYTHING

7 Story:
Pup-Fu Power

25 Story:
King for a Day

47 Story:
Ice Team

65 PAWsome
Activities

PaRragon

Bath • New York • Cologne • Melbourne • Delhi
Hong Kong • Shenzhen • Singapore

Pup-Fu Power

It was a special day for Farmer Yumi's martial arts students. The PAW Patrol, Mayor Goodway and Chickaletta were all gathered in Farmer Yumi's barn, eager to earn their Pup-Fu yellow belts.

"Students, are you ready?" asked Farmer Yumi. The pups quickly lined up and then bowed to their sensei.

9

One by one, the pups showed off their moves. Rocky twirled a staff and Marshall span around. Skye kicked high and Rubble stood tall. Zuma was ready for action.

Then Chase announced, "And now I will – ah ... ah ... CHOO! I'm sorry. I'm allergic to ... *kittens*?"

The Kit-tastrophe Crew from Foggy Bottom
had sneaked into Farmer Yumi's barn!

Mayor Humdinger had brought his team of mischievous kittens to prove that Cat-Jitsu was better than Pup-Fu.

"Pup-Fu rules! Cat-Jitsu drools!" Mayor Goodway said, folding her arms. "And there's nothing like Hen-Kido!"

"Bwok!" Chickaletta clucked in agreement and gave a quick kick.

"It's not about which art is superior," Farmer Yumi said. "The point is for all pups, kittens, mayors and chickens to do their best."

Mayor Humdinger clapped his hands and his Kit-tastrophe Crew sprang into action. They jumped and kicked and rolled on balls of wool. One kitten headed for the zip line.

"I'll show you how a Pup-Fu master uses the zip line," Marshall said as he jumped up and grabbed the cord. "Wheeee!"

The mischievous kitten hooked a mechanical claw onto the line and gave it a good shake.

Ziiing! Marshall went flying!

Marshall crashed to the ground.
"Are you okay?" Rubble asked.
"Yeah," Marshall replied. "A Pup-Fu
master always knows exactly how
to land when they fall."
"For the next part of our belt test,
we'll have sparring," Farmer Yumi said.

The pups and kittens began to spar. Marshall and a kitten in blue bowed and then sprang into action. Marshall jumped and spun through the air. The kitten launched a ball of wool from her pack.

"Whoa!" Marshall yelped as he fell
to the floor. His legs were wrapped in wool.
"Pup-Fu?" Mayor Humdinger snickered.
"That looks like pup fail!"

19

It was time to award the belts. Farmer Yumi gave each pup a golden yellow belt. She was proud of them and their dedication to Pup-Fu. "Your extra-hard work would please the ancient masters."

But there were no belts for the kittens.

"Mayor Humdinger," Farmer Yumi said, "until your kittens learn to control themselves and their tools, I'm afraid they cannot earn their yellow belts."

"Hooray for the PAW Patrol!" Ryder cheered.
They were all good pups — and they were all
very good sports.

The End

King for a Day

One sunny day, the PAW Patrol pups were practising for a play. They all dressed up in costumes and tried out their lines.

Chase was going to play the role of the king. The other pups were going to be his brave knights.

Meanwhile, Cap'n Turbot was busy building a stage for the pups' play. He had put the floor, scenery and castle into place and was almost finished. But just as he hammered one last nail into the castle door …

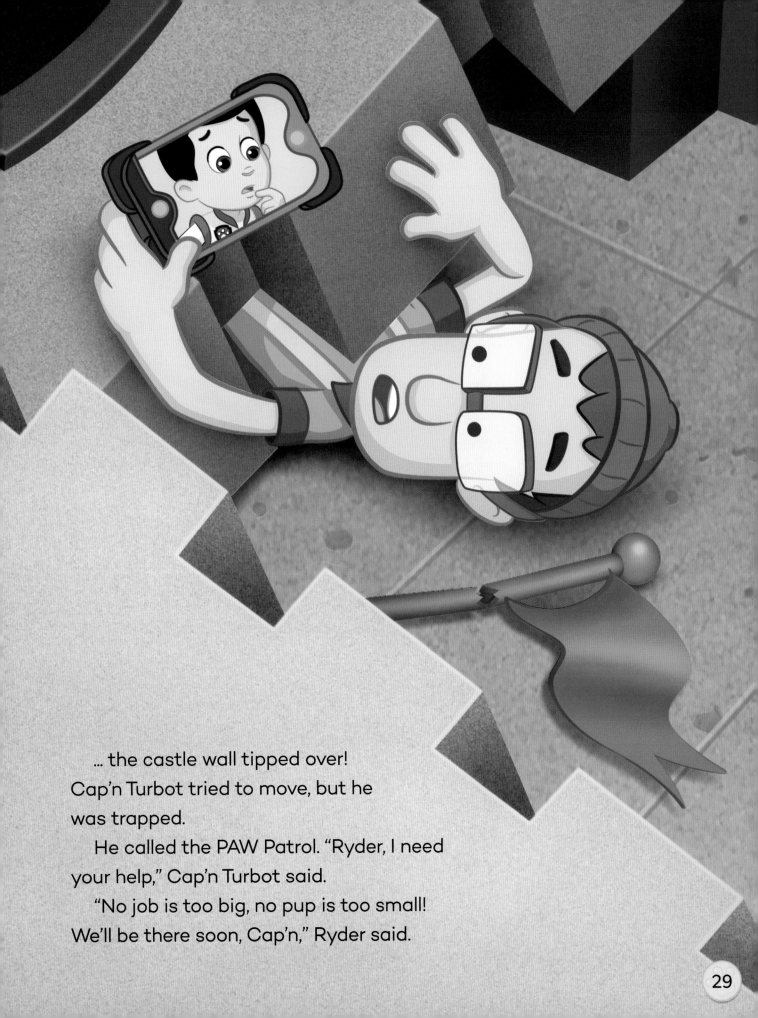

... the castle wall tipped over!
Cap'n Turbot tried to move, but he
was trapped.

He called the PAW Patrol. "Ryder, I need
your help," Cap'n Turbot said.

"No job is too big, no pup is too small!
We'll be there soon, Cap'n," Ryder said.

Ryder and the pups raced to the rescue.
"Thank goodness you're here!" said
Cap'n Turbot when the PAW Patrol arrived.

Ryder quickly gave each
pup an important job to do.

Rubble used the crane arm on his digger to lift the castle wall.

Next, Chase pulled the castle tower away, freeing
Cap'n Turbot.
"Good job, pups!" Ryder said. "Now we need to make
sure you're not hurt, Cap'n."

Marshall used his X-ray screen to check Cap'n Turbot over. Luckily, the Cap'n didn't have any broken bones.

Then Ryder and the pups got to work fixing the castle.

Using her helicopter, Skye lifted one of the walls back into place.

"This pup's got to fly!" said Skye.

Rocky used his mechanical screwdriver to attach the door to the wall. "Don't lose it, reuse it!" he barked.

Finally, Marshall and Ryder painted
the castle in shades of pink and purple.

The castle was soon finished, and the pups' play could start.
But suddenly Chase began to cough.

Marshall gave Chase a quick check-up and realized the pup was sick.

"Marshall, would you be able to play the king instead?" Ryder asked.

"Yes, sir!" Marshall said.

So the play began. It was the story of a princess,
played by Cali the cat, trapped in a tall tower.
Only a king could save her.
     The pup who could pull the bone out from
the stone would become king.

When it was Marshall's turn, he
pulled the bone out easily. It flew
out of his paws and hit the castle.
The princess fell from the tower!

Marshall moved quickly and caught
the princess. Cali purred happily.

Lady Skye placed a crown on top of Marshall's head. "Good job, King Marshall," she said.

"Hooray! The king saved the day.
And Marshall saved the play!"
Ryder said.

The End

Ice Team

The PAW Patrol was getting ready for a trip to see their friend Jake at the ice fields. Suddenly, there was a loud roar, and a big truck rolled up.

"Presenting the PAW Patroller!" Ryder said. "It's a Lookout on wheels. It can take us anywhere. And Robo-dog will be our driver!"

A door opened in the side and a mechanical dog hopped out.

As Ryder was showing the pups around the PAW Patroller, Jake called.

"Hi, Jake! How are the ice fields?" Ryder asked.

"Amazing!" Jake said. "Take a look." The screen showed snowy hills and an icy river.

Just then, Jake slipped on the ice and the pups could hear him cry, "My phone! My maps! All of my stuff!"
Jake's equipment had fallen into the icy river!

"Jake's in big trouble!" Rubble barked.

"Pups, get your vehicles," Ryder said.

The PAW Patroller's back door opened and a ramp came out. The pups quickly drove their vehicles on board. Robo-dog started the engine and the PAW Patroller rolled into action.

At the ice fields, Jake was trying to get his backpack out of the water. But the river bank was so icy that he began to slide in! Luckily, a husky pup pulled him out.

"Sweet save!" Jake said, and then he introduced himself.

"I'm Everest," the pup replied. "I rescued someone! I've always wanted to do a real rescue."

"We should probably get going," Everest said. "A storm's rolling in. I wouldn't want to lose my first real rescue in a blizzard. We can wait it out in my igloo. To get there, we can do this...."

Everest flopped onto her belly and slid down the hill.

"Belly-bogganing!" Jake said, taking off after her. "Look out below!"

The two new friends slid along on the ice, zooming past some penguins.

When the PAW Patroller reached the ice fields, the snow was falling hard. The team started to look for Jake. They found his frozen phone and pack.

"This means Jake doesn't have any supplies," Ryder said. Then he noticed something in the snow. "Are those tracks?"

Chase gave the tracks a sniff. "That's Jake, all right! And he's got another pup with him."

"Those tracks should lead us to Jake," Ryder said. "Let's follow them."

As Chase followed the tracks on
the ground, Skye took to the frosty air.

Everest and Jake came to a narrow bridge that stretched across a deep, dark ravine. "My igloo is just across that ice bridge," Everest said.

"Will it hold us?" Jake asked.

"I hope so," the husky replied. "It's the only way to get over."

As they walked across, they heard a terrible cracking noise. The ice bridge was breaking!

Just as the bridge collapsed, Skye swooped in, catching Jake and Everest with a rope. But before she had carried them to the other side of the ravine, the rope broke.

"Jump!" Jake yelled to Everest.

Everest landed on a ledge, but Jake missed it.
He caught the edge with his fingers and
dangled dangerously over the dark ravine.

"Don't worry!" Everest yelled. "I've got you!"
She snagged Jake's sleeve and pulled him to
safety. "Yes! Two rescues in one day!"

Everyone went to Jake's cabin on the mountain for toasted marshmallows – and a surprise.

"Everest," Jake said, "I could use a smart pup like you to help out on the mountain."

"And for saving Jake and showing great rescue skills," Ryder added, "I'd like to make you an official member of the PAW Patrol!"

"This is the best day ever!" Everest said, and all the pups cheered.

The End

PAW PATROL™

PAWsome Activities

When there's trouble in Adventure Bay,
PAW Patrol is ready for action!

"I'm ready to fight blazes,"
says Marshall, the brave fire pup.

"I'm always on patrol!" says Chase,
the police dog.

"My shovel often comes in handy,"
barks Rubble, the construction pup.

"I love the view of Adventure Bay from up in my helicopter," says Skye, the fearless pilot pup.

"I can find a use for anything," barks Rocky,
PAW Patrol's top recycler.

"I like to make a splash!" says Zuma,
the water-loving labrador.

Ryder is the PAW Patrol leader. He and the pups
are always ready to save the day.

The PAW Patrol love to visit Katie
at the Pup Parlour.

Katie's cat, Cali, is the purr-fect pet.

SKYE

Chase can race to the rescue
in his PAWsome police truck.

Whenever someone's in trouble, Marshall jumps in his fire truck to save the day.

Rocky's recycling truck is the perfect vehicle
to help him move other people's rubbish.

Rubble has a big digger that
comes with a drill and a shovel.

Skye can fly over Adventure Bay in her helicopter and keep an eye out for anyone in trouble.

Zuma zooms over the water in his hovercraft,
ready to reach an emergency at sea.

Ryder drives a hi-tech ATV. It can turn
into a jet ski or a snowmobile, too!

Draw a line to connect each food bowl to the correct pup.

1

2

3

4

5

6

a

b

c

d

e

f

The pups deserve some treats.
How many dog biscuits can you count?

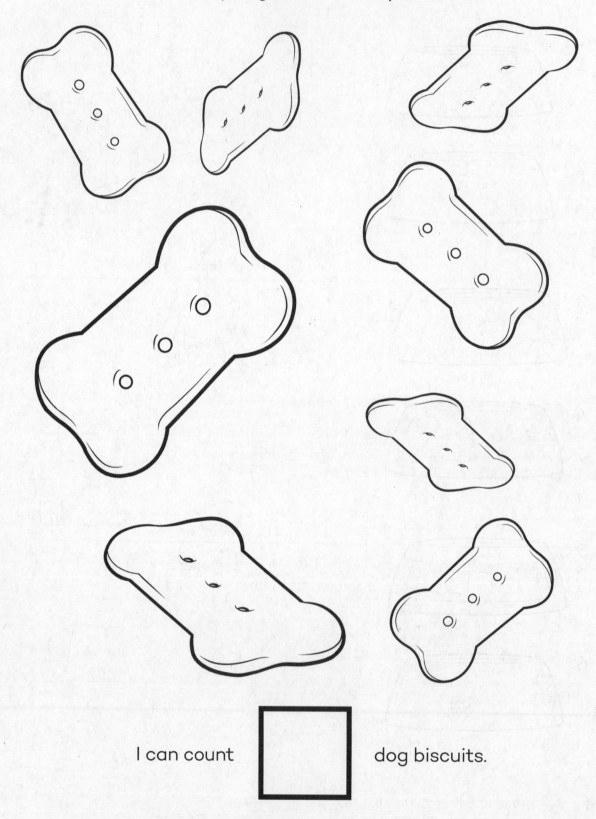

I can count ☐ dog biscuits.

Look at these two pictures of Ryder's PupPad.
Can you circle five differences in the bottom picture?

85

It's Halloween and the PAW Patrol are having a party!
Skye is a PAWsome princess.

Ryder is dressed as a brave knight.

Zuma loves the water, so a pirate
costume is the perfect choice for him.

Rubble is ready to sing like a famous
pop star for some trick-or-treat sweets.

Marshall is dressed as a pumpkin.

Katie and Cali have joined the pups' party. They're a little scared by the pups' Halloween outfits!

Rocky looks amazing in his costume.

Chase is bobbing for apples.
How many apples can you count?

I can count ☐ apples.

93

Captain Zuma is sailing across the high seas.

Oops! Careful, Marshall!

Spot and circle the Halloween-themed objects.

Answer:

The PAW Patrol is having so much fun.
They all love Halloween and dressing up!

Today, Marshall is training to run
Adventure Bay's Fire Rescue Course.

The pups cheer on their friend.

Marshall runs and leaps and – oops!
He trips on a log.

Next, Marshall gets his paws tangled up
in the tyre obstacle.

"Here I come, Cali!" calls Marshall.
"Ladder up and – oh no!"
Marshall's cat rescue isn't going to plan ...

... he falls off the ladder.
"I'm not going to break any fire pup
records today," says Marshall.

"It looks like Marshall could use a helping hand," says Ryder. "PAW Patrol to the Lookout!"

"We have an emergency," says Ryder.
"And that emergency is Marshall.
He needs our help!"

"Marshall, we just want you to try your best and not worry about breaking the record."

"Rocky, I need you to fix Marshall's ladder," says Ryder.

"Marshall, I need you and your fire gear ready to do your best."

"I'll try to do my best ... and forget about the rest," barks Marshall.

"I can use this broom handle to make rungs for Marshall's ladder," says Rocky.

"Good work, Rocky," says Ryder.

On the day of the race, Chase helps Marshall
get to the starting line on time.

"My cones will stop traffic until Marshall gets here," says Chase.

"Good morning, Adventure Bay!"
says Mayor Goodway.

"Today, Marshall will try to run the
Fire Rescue Course in record time!"

"I'll do my best and forget the rest," says Marshall.

"Ready! Set! Go!"
Mayor Goodway shouts.

117

Marshall almost trips during the tyre obstacle challenge. "I'm okay," he says.

Marshall completes the animal rescue without a problem!

"He's making really good time,"
says Ryder. "Go, Marshall!"

Marshall shoots water from his fire hose and hits the target.

"Now I just have to get to the finish line!" says Marshall.

Uh-oh! The cameraman accidentally knocks over a light and starts a fire.

Marshall stops racing
to put out the fire.

When the fire is safely out, Marshall runs
as fast as he can to the finish line.

Oh no! Marshall didn't get the record.

"That's okay," Marshall says. "I did my best."

"Because you stopped to put out a real fire,
you're an Adventure Bay Hero," the mayor says.

Hooray for Marshall, the greatest fire pup in the world!

Circle the picture of Marshall that
is different from the others.

a

b

c

d

Marshall is looking through the big telescope. He hopes that a flock of geese will return to Adventure Bay soon.

131

Do you see a goose? Circle it.

132

Rocky builds a nest for tired geese,
and Rubble fills the nest with bread.

"Looks like the geese are here," says Ryder.

Help Marshall find
the baby goose.

Start

Finish

Answer:

135

"Fuzzy is a good name for you,"
Marshall tells the baby goose.

"Looks like you have a new BGFF –
Best Goose Friend Forever," says Skye.

137

Draw a picture of your best friend.

Marshall washes his fire truck.

Fuzzy dries the windows.

Marshall makes sure that Fuzzy
gets enough to eat.

Marshall trips on his food bowl
and Fuzzy does, too!

Fuzzy wants Marshall to sleep
outside with the geese.

143

Good night, Fuzzy.

Fuzzy wakes up before Marshall and wanders off to eat breadcrumbs.

"Fuzzy is gone!" says Marshall. "We have to find him before his flock leaves."

"PAW Patrol, to the Lookout!"

Zuma and Skye get Ryder's alert
and their dog tags light up.

Rubble and Rocky race to the Lookout.

Draw a line to connect each badge to the correct pup.

1

2

3

4

a

b

c

d

Draw a big fire hat for Marshall.

"Chase is on the case!"

"This pup's gotta fly!"

"Rocky to the rescue!"

"Rubble on the double!"

"Let's dive in!"

PAW Patrol is at the Lookout.

"PAW Patrol, ready for action, Ryder, sir!" says Chase.

"Marshall's friend Fuzzy is missing," says Ryder.
"We have to find him!"

"Chase, we'll need your megaphone to call Fuzzy," says Ryder.

Marshall will help look, too.

Draw a line to connect each
pup to their vehicle.

1

2

3

4

a

b

c

d

PAW Patrol is on a roll! Use the key
to help you colour in the picture.

Key		
1	=	yellow
2	=	brown
3	=	green
4	=	red
5	=	blue
6	=	pink
7	=	grey

2

1

6

4

6

6

3

5

7

7

The search for Fuzzy begins!

Chase calls for Fuzzy on his megaphone. "Honk! Honk!"

Can you work out which picture of Chase
is different from the others? Circle it!

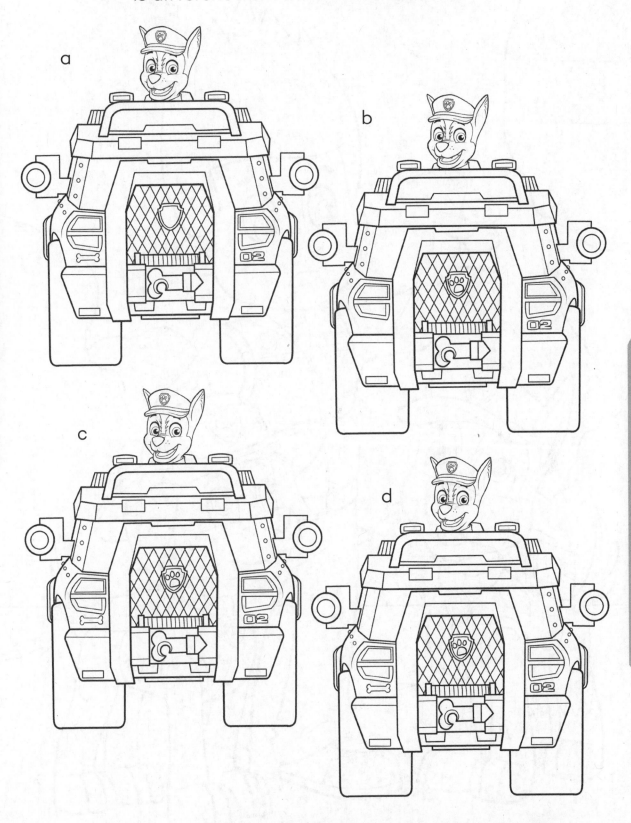

a

b

c

d

Marshall finds one of Fuzzy's feathers. Chase gives it a sniff.

"Achoo! I'm a little allergic to feathers," says Chase.

Chase is on the case! Use the key
to help you colour in the picture.

Key		
1	=	blue
2	=	yellow
3	=	brown
4	=	red
5	=	black

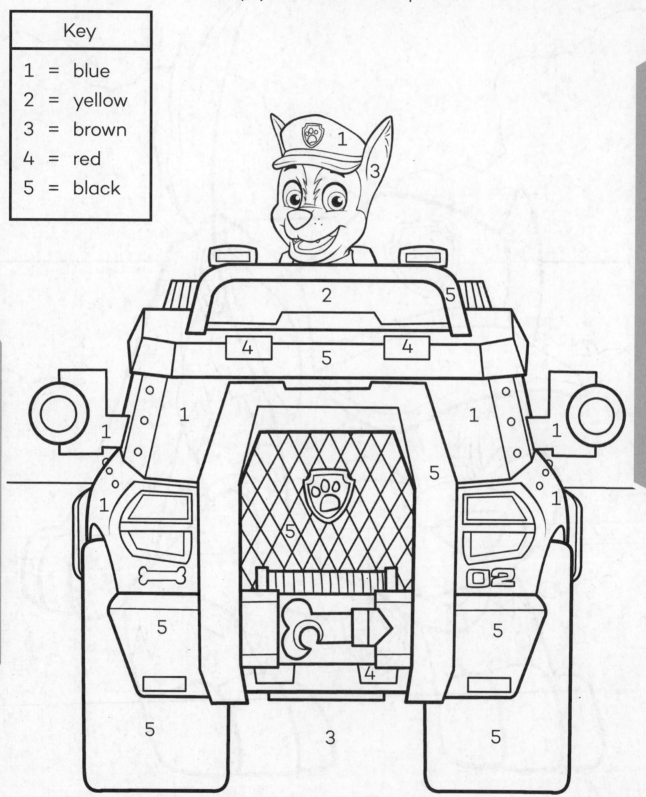

Help Marshall find Fuzzy!

Start

Finish

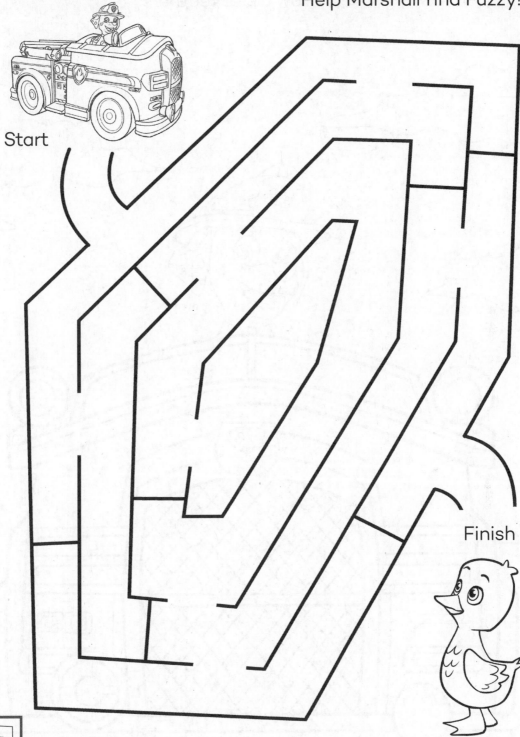

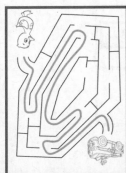

Answer:

171

Follow those feathers!

Oh no! A big seagull is picking on Fuzzy and Fuzzy can't fly away because he's trapped in a plastic ring.

Chase's net takes care of the seagull.

"Marshall, use your ladder to climb up to Fuzzy," says Ryder.

Marshall rescues Fuzzy.

"Great job!" says Ryder.

Chase and Marshall are a terrific team!

"The geese are flying away!" says Ryder.
"Fuzzy has to catch up with them."

Fuzzy doesn't want to leave Marshall.

"If Fuzzy doesn't leave now, he'll never catch up with the other geese," says Ryder. "Wait, I have an idea!"

Ryder puts a special flying vest on Marshall.

The vest is tied to Skye's helicopter.
Skye takes off, lifting Marshall with her.

Skye is ready to fly! Use the key to help you colour in the picture.

Key	
1 =	pink
2 =	brown
3 =	tan
4 =	silver
5 =	blue

5

1

3

3

2

2

3

3

2

1

3

4

3

1

3

4

1

3

3

5

Marshall is flying! Fuzzy is following him.

Marshall and Fuzzy catch up with the geese.

186

Draw Fuzzy flying with his friends.

"Bye, Fuzzy, you silly goose!" says Marshall.

"Great work, pups. You did a really
good job today," says Ryder.

"Hooray for the PAW Patrol!" barks Rocky.

Rocky to the rescue! Use the key to help you colour in the picture.

Key

1 = yellow
2 = orange
3 = green
4 = grey
5 = blue

Whenever there's trouble, just yelp for help!